THE 100TH
GREATEST DAY
OF SCHOOL

BY MICHELLE POPLOFF
ILLUSTRATED BY BILL BASSO

SCHOLASTIC INC.

New York   Toronto   London   Auckland   Sydney

Mexico City   New Delhi   Hong Kong   Buenos Aires

To my dear friend Alyce Curry
For all you do . . . this one's for you.
—M. P.

For Dad.
—B. B.

ISBN-13: 978-0-439-24405-3
ISBN-10: 0-439-24405-6

12 11 10 9 8 7 6 5   10 11 12/0

Printed in the U.S.A.   40
First Scholastic printing, January 2002

CONTENTS

Chapter 1
DOWN IN THE DUMPS

Mrs. Bono put down the chalk and looked at her class.

"No one is listening," she said. "What's wrong? You all look down in the dumps."

Wanda Doomsday's hand shot up.

"Every day is so gloomy and gray."

Wanda's friend Helen Hooper agreed.

"This time of year is snoring, boring."

The class laughed.

"The weather makes me slumpy and grumpy," added Buffy.

"Don't forget mopey and dopey," said Hector.

Wayne yawned. "And sleepy." He looked right at Wanda. "And creepy."

"All right," said their teacher. "I'm glad you still have some energy." She pointed to the calendar. "Who knows what special day is coming up? It only comes once a year."

When no one could guess, Mrs. Bono wrote it on the board:

THE 100th DAY OF SCHOOL!

"Let's have a 100th day of school party!" said Buffy.

"We'll all bring in 100 of something," said Helen.

"Carrying 100 things to school will be hard work," said Wayne.

"Choose something easy," said Mrs. Bono. "I have an old button collection. I'll bring 100 buttons to school."

"I know what I'm bringing," said Buffy. "And I'm not telling."

"Good idea," said Mrs. Bono. "Everyone keep what you're bringing a secret. Then we'll all be surprised on the 100th school day. But if you're not sure about something, please ask before you bring it in." Mrs. Bono circled the big day on the calendar.

Everyone was excited.

Everyone except Wanda Doomsday.

Chapter 2
WORRYWART WANDA

Wanda was worried.

She didn't have a collection of 100 of anything at home.

There might be 100 dust balls under her bed, but Granny wouldn't let her bring them.

What could she bring to school?

Wanda looked around.

The leaves had blown off the trees.

There were ugly rocks on the ground.

Too boring. Too heavy.

Maybe her brother, Artie, or Granny would have an idea.

Artie was stuffing his face with Granny's
batty brownies when Wanda walked in.
She poured some milk to drink with
her brownie.

Granny was talking on the telephone.
"Of course we're coming tomorrow,
Auntie Zelma," Granny said. "We'll
bring some good ones. Be sure you have
some, too. Toodle-oo!"

"What are we bringing Great-Auntie Zelma?" asked Artie.

"Riddles, of course," said Granny. "She got me started with spooky riddles, and I passed them down to you and Wanda."

"I like visiting Auntie Zelma at the senior center," said Wanda. "Maybe she'll have an idea for my school project."

"Which project is that?" Granny asked.
"I need to bring something to celebrate the 100th day of school," said Wanda. "What are some of the other children bringing?" asked Granny.

"It's supposed to be a surprise," Wanda replied. "Helen has a stamp collection, and Kim collects shells. That's what they'll probably bring." She took a long drink of milk. "I want to bring something special."

Granny patted Wanda's shoulder. "You'll think of something, dearie. Right now, let's think of some riddles for Great-Auntie Zelma."

Chapter 3
THAT SPECIAL SOMEONE

"Auntie Zelma," said Granny Doomsday,
"you look terrific. I love your new hairdo."
"Guess where I had it done?" Auntie
Zelma asked.

"Where?" asked Artie.

"At the *boo*-ty parlor," Auntie Zelma
cackled.

"You're starting early with the jokes,"
said Artie.

"No point in waiting at my age," said
Auntie Zelma with a laugh.

"How old are you anyway?" Wanda asked.

"Wanda Lucille!" cried Granny. "You shouldn't ask Auntie Zelma her age." "Why not?" asked Auntie Zelma. "I'll be 100 this month, and that's no joke." "Cool!" said Artie.

"Did you say 100?" asked Wanda.
"Abso-toot-a-loot-ly," said Auntie
Zelma. She turned to Artie. "What
instrument does a skeleton play in the
school band?"
Artie scratched his head.
"I'm not sure," he said.

20

"The trom-*bone*," Auntie Zelma said, slapping Artie's knee. "That's called a knee-slapper!"

"Here's one for you, Auntie Zelma," said Artie. "Did you hear whom the vampire married?"

"Who?" she asked.

"The *ghoul necks*-door," Artie answered.

"That's grand, Artie," giggled Auntie Zelma. "A doubleheader joke. How about you, Wanda? What kind of tests does a vampire teacher give his class?"

Wanda shrugged.

"Blood tests," Auntie Zelma said, poking Wanda's ribs with her bony elbow.

Wanda tried to smile.

"What's wrong, Wanda?" asked Auntie Zelma. "No riddles for me?"

For once, Wanda couldn't think of a riddle. All she could think of was that magic number.

"Did you say 100?" Wanda asked again, an idea forming in her head.

"Yes, yes, yes," said Auntie Zelma. "I'll be 100 years young in a few more days."

Wanda jumped up and almost landed in Auntie Zelma's lap.

"Will you please come to class with me to celebrate the 100th day of school?" she asked.

"How's that, dearie?" asked Auntie Zelma.

"Everyone has to bring 100 of something," Wanda explained. "I want to bring you. You're better than 100 pencils or paper clips any day."

"You bet I am!" said Auntie Zelma.

"You're 100 all rolled into one!" Wanda shouted.

"Wanda," said Artie, "you've had some
weird ideas before, but this one takes
the cake."

Great-Auntie Zelma smacked her lips.
"Cake? Did you say cake?" she asked.

Wanda clapped her brother on the back.
"Good point, Artie," she said. "I'll bring
a birthday cake with 100 candles."
"You'll burn down the school," he said.
"We'll just light one for good luck,"
said Wanda.
Granny Doomsday held up her hand.
"First ask your teacher," she said. "Then
I'll speak with Mrs. Curry here at the
senior center. I don't want this to be too
much for Auntie Zelma."
"Nonsense, dearie," Auntie Zelma said,
shivering a little.
"Are you cold, Auntie Zelma?" asked
Wanda.
"Not at all," Auntie Zelma said with a
smile. "I'm just excited about my
brrr-thday party!"

Chapter 4
THE COUNTDOWN CONTINUES

Now Wanda was looking forward to the 100th day of school more than anyone else.

Most of the kids had been able to keep what they were bringing a secret.

Finally it was the 99th day of school.

"Wanda, I have to talk to you," Helen said. She looked worried.

"What's wrong, Helen?" asked Wanda.

"I heard the boys talking," Helen said.
"Hector was bragging about bringing
something that no one has ever brought
to school before. He said it's really the
greatest thing for our 100th day party."

"Great, huh?" said Wanda. "Well, I'm
bringing something greater. And I mean
great."

"I'm just warning you, Wanda," said
Helen. "I'm sure you're bringing
something much better."

Wanda nodded.

"You'll see tomorrow," she said.

That night, Wanda made a birthday
crown for Great-Auntie Zelma.
It glittered with 100 shiny stars.

Then Wanda made a matching crown
for herself.

Move over Hector, she thought.
*Tomorrow Auntie Zelma will star in
our 100th day of school celebration —
thanks to me!*

Chapter 5
THE 100TH DAY OF SCHOOL

When Wanda walked into her class with
Auntie Zelma, everyone looked up.
"Thank you for bringing your
great-aunt to our 100th day celebration,
Wanda," Mrs. Bono said. "Please sit in
my reading chair," she said to Auntie
Zelma. "It's very cozy."
While Wanda hung up their coats,
Wayne helped Auntie Zelma over to
Mrs. Bono's chair.

"Why, thank you, sonny," said Auntie
Zelma.

"You're welcome, and my name is Wayne."

"Rain? Did you say rain?" Auntie Zelma
sang, "*Rain, rain, go away! Don't rain
down on my birthday!*"

"You heard her," said Wanda. "Wayne,
Wayne, go away!"

She carefully placed the birthday crown
on Auntie Zelma's head. Wanda was
already wearing her own.

Just then there was a barking noise
outside the classroom.

"It's Hector," Buffy said, her eyes wide.
"And he has a dog."

Wanda stayed at Auntie Zelma's side.
She folded her arms.

"What's so great about Hector's dog?"
she mumbled.

"Please come in, Hector," said Mrs. Bono. "Would you like to begin our 100th day of school celebration?"

"All right," said Hector. "This is my dog, Gus. Gus is 100 years old in dog years. That makes him almost 15 in people years."

"What kind of dog is he?" Helen asked.

"He's a Great Dane, and he's a really great dog," said Hector. "Since Gus is 100, he's glad to be here for the 100th day of school."

All the kids clapped, even Wanda.

So that was Hector's great surprise, she thought. *His Great Dane, Gus.*

Gus walked over to Auntie Zelma and rested at her feet.

"Look at the cute puppy dog," said Auntie Zelma. "Wanda, dearie, will you give Gus your crown since he's 100, just like me?"

Wanda had no choice.

"Sure, Auntie Zelma," she said.

She bent down and put the crown on Gus's head.

The crown drooped over one eye.

Everyone laughed and clapped some more.

"Wanda," said Mrs. Bono. "Since all eyes are on Gus and your great-aunt, you may go next."

Wanda nodded.

"This is my Great-Auntie Zelma," she said proudly. "She's 100 years old."

"That's 100 years *young*," Auntie Zelma corrected her.

"Right," said Wanda. "I brought her to celebrate the 100th day of school."

Great-Auntie Zelma waved.

"*Howl* do you do?" she said.

The kids laughed.

Wanda smiled.

Maybe it's not so bad to share the 100th day spotlight with a dog, she thought.

Chapter 6
HAPPY BIRTHDAY!

Later that afternoon, Hector walked over and sat down next to Gus and Auntie Zelma.

"You are a very *haunt*-some young man," Auntie Zelma said to Hector. "Why, if I were younger, you could sweep me off my feet."

Hector blushed.

Wanda coughed.

There was no stopping Auntie Zelma once she got started.

"What color is a chilly ghost?" Auntie
Zelma asked Hector.

"I'm not sure," he said.

"*Boo!*" shouted Auntie Zelma.

Hector jumped. Gus snored.

Auntie Zelma pointed a bony finger at
Wayne.

"Come closer, sonny," she said.

Wayne stepped forward.

"Knock, knock," she said.

"Who's there?" asked Wayne.

"Gus," she said.

Wayne looked at Gus, the dog.

"Gus who?" he asked.

"Gus whose birthday it is!" laughed
Auntie Zelma.

Wanda laughed, too.

"Mrs. Bono," she said, "can we sing
'Happy Birthday' now?"

"Certainly," said Mrs. Bono.

She carried the cake over to
Great-Auntie Zelma.

"The cake has 101 candles on it,"
said Wanda. "The extra candle is for
good luck."
Wanda looked at Gus, snoring away.
"This is for both of you," she said.
Great-Auntie Zelma smiled that special
Doomsday smile.
"One . . . two . . . three!" said Mrs. Bono.
Then the class began to sing.
"*Happy birthday to you!*
You're 100, it's true!
We're happy to know you!
Happy birthday to you."
Great-Auntie Zelma made a wish and
blew out the one candle that was lit.
Everyone clapped and cheered.

"Here's a birthday box filled with 100 of my favorite riddles," Wanda said to Auntie Zelma. "I guess I did have a collection after all."

"Thank you, dearie. I always say a riddle a day keeps the doctor away," she cackled.

"You get the first piece of cake, Auntie Zelma," said Wanda.

"Well, just a tiny piece. I always had a sweet tooth," said Auntie Zelma. "Now that tooth is all I have left!"

The kids laughed again.

"I enjoyed my visit today and hope you'll invite me back for my next birthday," Auntie Zelma said.

"But," said Buffy, "you won't be 100 next year."

"No problem," said Wanda. "Next year we'll celebrate the 101st day of school."

"Hooray!" the class cheered.

Mrs. Bono gave Wanda a double thumbs-up.

"It's a deal," said Auntie Zelma. "I'll bring a bone for the dog and more jokes for the kids.

"Which reminds me," she said.

"What did the vampire say at the end of the 100th day of school?"

"What?" the class called out.

Auntie Zelma smiled.

"I'll see you *necks* year!"

48